Items on loan can be renewed by phone
or Internet. Call 0845 230 3232 or
visit our website.

Buckinghamshire
libraryservice
CULTURE AND LEARNING

www.buckscc.gov.uk/libraries

D1439870

With special thanks to Alex and Chris

With thanks to our readers:

Pippa Armitage
Max Craven
C. Heywood
Daniel Khan
Marcus P. Riley
Kyle Smith

First published in 2009 in Great Britain by
Barrington Stoke Ltd
18 Walker St, Edinburgh, EH3 7LP

www.barringtonstoke.co.uk

ISBN: 978-1-84299-693-5

Printed in Great Britain by Bell & Bain Ltd

Contents

Chapter 1
"I've called the police"

"Quick, hide!" said Leon to Dom.

Leon's mum was spying on them from the kitchen window.

Dom hid behind a wheelie bin.

Dom was Leon's best mate. But Leon's mum didn't like him. She always said, "That Dom is bad news!"

Leon had tried to tell her. "Mum, I know he *looks* big and a bully. But he's OK really. He's a good guy!"

But it was no use. Leon's mum had made up her mind about Dom. She told Leon to stay away from him.

"You can come out now," Leon told Dom. "Mum's gone."

Dom came out from behind the wheelie bin. He and Leon walked down the street. People rushed past Dom, some even crossed the street as if Dom was going to rob them.

What are they afraid of? Leon said to himself. They just didn't know Dom like Leon did.

Leon and Dom were walking past a wire fence. On the other side was a rubbish tip. Seagulls were making a big din, screaming and fighting over the rubbish.

Dom and Leon saw a boy by the fence.

"What's that kid doing?" said Dom.

Then they saw that the boy had an air gun. He was aiming it at the gulls.

4

A big gull came swooping past.

"Crack, crack," went the gun.

The gull fell out of the sky.

The boy had shot it. But it was still
alive. It flapped about on the ground. The
boy was aiming the air gun to shoot it again.

Dom walked up to the boy. He took the air gun off him and threw it over the fence into the tip.

"Go away!" Dom said to the boy. "Before I get really mad."

The boy took one look at Dom's grim face and ran away.

"I'm going to take a look at that gull," said Dom.

"Careful," said Leon. All over the fence it said, "DANGER! KEEP OUT!"

But Dom got over the wire into the tip. A man driving a JCB saw him. He shouted, "Hey, you! You shouldn't be in here!" He got out his mobile.

Dom jumped down into the tip. He ran to the hurt gull. It pecked him when he tried to pick it up. Leon saw blood on Dom's hands.

"I've called the police!" yelled the JCB
driver. He got in his JCB and began to drive
over the tip to where Dom was bending over
the gull.

"Run!" yelled Leon. That JCB was getting
closer.

The gull had stopped pecking Dom. It lay
very still. Its eyes were shut.

Leon shouted, "Leave it. It's dead!"

But Dom wouldn't leave the gull. He picked it up. He put it inside the front pocket of his hoodie. Then he started to get back over the fence. The JCB guy had got out of his cab! He was running towards Dom, shaking his fist.

"Hurry up!" Leon yelled to Dom. "He'll catch you!"

Dom jumped from the top of the fence.

"Quick! Quick!" yelled Leon. He could hear police sirens. They were very close. Were the police coming to get him and Dom?

Dom and Leon raced away from the tip. The JCB driver found the air gun. He picked it up.

"Have you been shooting birds?" he yelled after them. "You cruel kids! Can't you find something better to do!"

Leon couldn't run any more. His legs felt like jelly. It felt like his heart was about to explode. But they were safe now. They were a long way from the tip. And he couldn't hear police sirens any more.

"I think that gull really is dead now," Leon told Dom.

"No, it isn't," said Dom.

"It looks dead to me," said Leon.

The gull's head was hanging out of Leon's hoodie. It had blood on its white feathers. Its eyes were closed.

Dom put his hand in his hoodie. "It isn't dead yet," he said. "I can feel its heart beating."

Leon didn't like even looking at the gull. All that blood made him feel sick. Anyway, what could they do to help it?

"Leave it here," Leon begged Dom. He didn't want anything to do with it. He wanted to walk away and just forget about it.

But Dom wouldn't walk away.

"No!" said Dom. "I'm not going to leave it. If we leave it here it's going to die."

"But what are you going to do with it?" asked Leon.

"I'm going to take it home," said Dom.

Chapter 2
Dom's Big Secret

Leon and Dom took the gull to the shed in Dom's garden.

Leon had never been into Dom's shed before.

"Wow!" said Leon, when they went in. Everywhere he looked, there were cages

with wild birds in them. A white dove cooed.
An owl gazed at him with big golden eyes.

"What are they doing here?" Leon asked
Dom.

"They have all been hurt," said Dom. "A
cat got that dove. That owl was hit by a car.
People find them and bring them to me."

"To you?" said Leon, puzzled. "Why do people bring them to you?"

"Because they know I'll look after them," said Dom. "I make them better. Then I let them go."

Leon was amazed. "I never knew you were a bird doctor!" Dom had kept that a big secret.

"I can't always make them better," said Dom, sadly. "I try my best. But sometimes they die anyway."

"Will the gull die?" asked Leon.

Dom shook his head. "I don't know," he said.

Dom put the bird on the table.

His big hands were really gentle. First, he disinfected the hurt wing with cotton wool and Dettol. Then he took out the air gun pellets with tweezers. He picked up some cardboard and a pair of scissors.

"What are you doing now?" asked Leon.

"I'm making a splint to tape to the gull's wing," said Dom, busy cutting out.

"Hey, could I do that?" asked Leon.

Dom shook his head. "No way!" he said. "I know what I'm doing. Anyone else who finds a bird that's hurt must take it to the vet's at once."

Dom had cut two wing shapes out of the cardboard. He put one each side of the gull's broken wing, and taped them into place. Then he taped the wing to the bird's body so it couldn't move it.

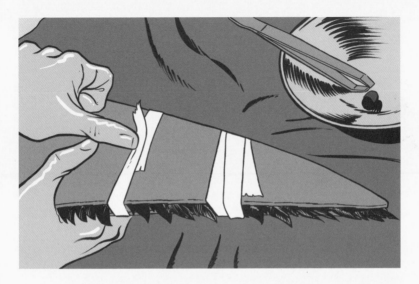

"You're good at that!" said Leon, amazed at Dom's skill. "That's a really neat job!"

But Dom looked worried. "The gull's very badly hurt," he told Leon. "I think it might die."

"Don't say that!" said Leon. Suddenly he cared about the sick gull. He wanted it to stay alive. He wanted it to fly again.

"Try to save it," he begged Dom.

Dom put the gull in a box. He put a bit of old blanket in to keep it warm.

The two boys sat and looked at the gull. Outside it was getting dark. But they didn't notice.

Suddenly, Leon said, "The gull's eyes are opening."

Dom got an eye dropper. He dropped some water into the gull's beak. The gull closed its eyes again. Its head flopped.

"It hasn't died, has it?" said Leon, in a panic.

"No," said Dom. He felt the gull's heart beat. "It's still alive. But only just."

Then Leon's mobile rang. It was his mum. She sounded really worried.

"Where are you?" she said. "Don't you know how late it is? You should have been home hours ago. Why didn't you call?"

"I'm busy," said Leon. "I'll come home soon."

"You'll come home right now!" said Mum. Then suddenly she asked, "You're not with that Dom are you?"

"No," lied Leon. "I'm not with Dom."

"You'd better not be!" said Mum. "He's a bad boy."

Leon gave a sigh. He switched off his phone. He wished Mum could see Dom right now, looking after the sick gull, trying to save its life. Then maybe she'd give Dom some respect.

"I've got to go home," Leon told Dom. "My mum's really mad with me. But I'll come back in the morning."

After Leon had gone, Dom stayed in the shed. He looked after the gull all that cold, dark night. He gave it water. He made sure it was kept warm.

At last the sky started getting light. The long night was over. But Dom was so worn out he fell asleep.

The shed door suddenly crashed open. Leon came racing in. "I came as soon as I could!" he said.

He saw Dom asleep in the chair. He saw the gull in the box, under the blanket. Its eyes were closed. It wasn't moving.

"Oh, no!" said Leon. "It died in the night!"

He didn't dare stroke the gull. He just stared sadly into the box. He gave Dom a shake and woke him up.

"What's the matter?" asked Dom, gazing round the room.

"The gull died," said Leon, going back to look into the box.

Dom jumped out of his chair and ran over. He put his hand into the box and stroked the gull's head.

Suddenly the gull opened its eyes. It lifted its head up. It tried to peck Dom with its sharp beak.

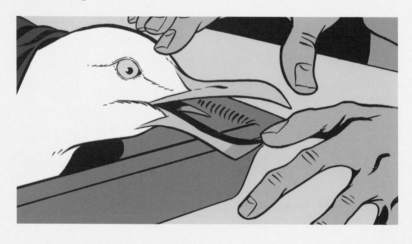

"Ow!" said Dom.

"It's alive!" said Leon, with a big smile on his face. He put his hand into the box.

"Hey, it's trying to peck me too. Stop it, gull, we're your mates."

"We should give it a name," said Dom.

Leon thought for a bit. "Why don't we call it Lucky?" he said.

"It got shot," said Dom. "It got a broken wing. I don't think it's very lucky."

"Yes, it is lucky," said Leon. "It's lucky because it met you, my mate Dom, the bird doctor."

Chapter 3
"Maybe he's better off dead!"

Lucky put up a brave fight. He didn't die after all. He stayed alive and grew stronger and stronger.

One day, Leon came rushing into Dom's shed. Dom was feeding Lucky cat food from a tin.

"It's time we let Lucky go," said Leon.

He wanted to see Lucky flying again, swooping about with the other gulls.

But Dom said, "Lucky's wing isn't better yet. We must make sure the bones are set."

A few days later, Leon said, "Lucky's wing must be better by now! When can we let him go?"

"We'll let him go in the morning," said Dom.

"Great!" said Leon. He couldn't wait. He thought, *Lucky will love it, being free again, flying about with his gull mates.*

Then Dom said, "Leon, I've got something to tell you."

"What is it?" said Leon. Dom's face looked grim, as if he had some really bad news to tell.

"Lucky might not be able to fly," said Dom. "He might never be able to fly again."

Leon couldn't believe it. He was really shocked. "I thought you fixed his wing!" he shouted.

"Fixing wings is hard," said Dom.
"Sometimes it works. Sometimes it doesn't.
If the bones don't set right, then the bird
can't fly."

"That's stupid!" shouted Leon. "I thought
you were a good bird doctor!"

Leon knew it was no use being angry with Dom. Dom had done his best. He tried not to panic.

He asked Dom, "What will Lucky do if he can't fly?"

"I'll have to keep him here," said Dom. "If he can't fly he'll get run over. Or a cat will get him. He'll be dead in no time."

Leon hated to think about it. A wild bird should be free. Not stuck in a cage for the rest of his life.

"If Lucky can't fly," muttered Leon to himself, "then maybe he's better off dead."

Chapter 4
Can Lucky Fly?

The next day Dom put Lucky inside the cardboard box.

"Where shall we let him go?" asked Leon.

"At the rubbish tip of course," said Dom. "That's where he lives. All his mates are there."

It was Sunday. There was no one around
at the tip. The JCB drivers didn't work at
the weekend. But Lucky's gull mates were
there, making a big din, screaming and
fighting over the rubbish. Dom and Leon got
over the fence.

Leon told Dom, "I didn't sleep last night.
I kept thinking, *will Lucky be able to fly?*"

Dom said, "I told you, maybe he won't."

Leon put his hands over his ears. He said, "I don't want to hear that. Stop saying that!"

Dom opened the box. Gently, he took the tape off Lucky's wing.

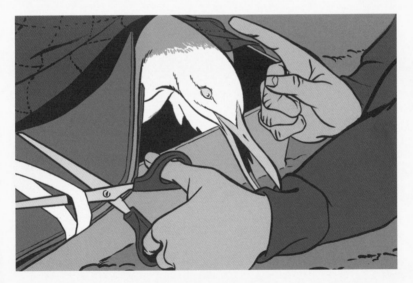

"Hey, stop pecking me," he told Lucky. "I'm trying to help you."

Dom took Lucky out of the box. He put him down on a pile of trash. Leon felt his heart thumping. He was so worried, he felt sick.

"Fly, Lucky," he said softly. "Go on, fly."

Lucky pecked at the trash. Then he hopped about. Then he flapped his bad wing. Then he fell over.

"His wing won't work!" said Leon. "It didn't set right!"

"Give him time," said Dom. But he looked worried too. He picked Lucky up. He put him back on his feet. "Try again, Lucky," he said.

Lucky tried to fly again. He flapped his wings. But he didn't take off.

"He can't fly!" Leon shouted. "Now he'll be in a cage for the rest of his life."

Leon felt his eyes getting wet. He didn't want to start crying. So he got angry. First he got angry at Dom.

"You're a useless bird doctor!" he yelled.

Then he got angry at Lucky.

"You useless bird!" he yelled, trying to blink back his tears. "Why can't you fly, you useless bird. What's the matter with you?"

Lucky flapped his wings again. Then suddenly he took off.

"He's flying!" shouted Dom as Lucky swooped away. "Look, he's flying!"

Leon's mouth fell open. It was all so sudden. Lucky was already just a dot in the blue sky.

"I can't see him any more. He's gone," said Leon. He didn't sound very happy.

"I thought you wanted him to fly," said Dom.

"I did," said Leon. "But he flew away so fast. I never got to say goodbye."

Chapter 5
Go, Lucky!

Leon and Dom walked back to Leon's house. Dom had the empty box in his hand. It still had Lucky's bit of blanket inside.

Leon told Dom, "Sorry I called you a useless bird doctor. I didn't mean it."

Dom said, "Forget about it. You were just worried about Lucky. Like I was."

Suddenly Leon said, "Oh, no."

There was his mum at the window. He'd forgotten all about her. Now she'd seen him with Dom. She looked really mad.

42

Leon's mum still thought Dom was a bad boy. But Leon had even more respect for Dom than ever.

"I'm going to tell Mum how you saved Lucky's life," Leon told Dom. "I'm going to tell her how you made him fly again. Then she'll have to change her mind about you."

"*Huh!*" said Dom. "I bet she doesn't."

"Well, I'm going to try anyway," said Leon. He looked again at Mum's angry face behind the window. "Maybe I'll tell her later," he told Dom, "when she's not so mad at me."

Dom and Leon went walking down the street. Leon heard a scream over their heads. A gull came swooping by.

"It's Lucky!" said Leon.

"How do you know?" grinned Dom. "All those gulls look the same."

"No, it's Lucky," said Leon. "See that? You left a bit of tape on his wing."

Lucky dived very low.

"He's come back to see us!" said Leon.

Lucky flew down the street with them
Then he gave one last scream and flew
slowly off over the rooftops.

Leon waved, "Go, Lucky!" he shouted.

He watched Lucky swoop away until he
got lost in a big white cloud of other gulls.
Then Leon ran to catch up with Dom with a
great big grin on his face.

Killer Croc

by
S. P. Gates

Levi is in Danger. There's a killer croc on
the loose – and it's hungry!
Can he escape its jaws?

You can order *Killer Croc* from our website at
www.barringtonstoke.co.uk

The Dunkirk Escape

by
Jim Eldridge

Dave Jones is trapped on the beach at
Dunkirk, as bombs explode all around him.
Can his son Tom get there in time to
save him?

You can order *The Dunkirk Escape* from our website at
www.barringtonstoke.co.uk

The Night Runner

by
Alan Combes

Greg trains at night to win the race.
But what's that spooky shape in the field?
Is it a ghost?

You can order *The Night Runner* from our website at
www.barringtonstoke.co.uk

Cliff Edge

by
Jane A. C. West

Can Danny make the climb of his life to
save his friend?
No ropes, no help – no hope?

You can order *Cliff Edge* from our website at
www.barringtonstoke.co.uk

United, Here I Come!

by
Alan Combes

Joey and Jimmy are very bad at football.
But Jimmy is sure he will play for United.
Is Jimmy crazy?